Mari Loves Mangoes

Author: Marva Carty

Illustrated by TullipStudio

(Paperback) ISBN 9781739832803

Illustrated by TullipStudio

Publisher's Name: MangoLime Publishing

Publisher's address: 27 Old Gloucester Street, London, WC1N 3AX

Acknowledgements

To Mummy and Daddy, Sis and Kahlil, thank you for your unwavering support.

To my worldwide hype squad, we did it!

Lastly, this book is for all my little adventurers across the diaspora. May you see yourself reflected in this small corner of fun and laughter.

Mari was excited for
the school holidays.

More time ...for hug ups with Mummy, Daddy and Carla...

..to relax with Brownie

and for trips
to the beach!

But the best thing is more time to eat
MANGOES!

Mari loves mangoes!
She may be small but she can eat them all!

Some are round
and orange,

Or long
and yellow

or big and red

But they ALL taste great!

Mari loves cold mango smoothies
when the sun is hot

She eats the green mangoes in spicy mango chow like Daddy
or baked fresh and warm in Mummy's yummy mango bread

Her favourite is a Julie mango picked
from her special tree in the garden.
Watch out though, the birds love them too!

Mari tries not to get mango juice all over her clothes so Mummy won't get upset.

But it doesn't always work.

And maybe just a bit more at dinner
so the rest don't get wasted.

Will there be mango treats at Keisha's party tomorrow?
Maybe a giant mango mousse cake with mango ice cream
If it's too much for everyone, she'll help Keisha out and bring
it home!

Mummy said, "That's enough, Mari. You'll spoil your appetite for the party tomorrow."

Mari cried, "But Mummy, mangoes are healthy fruits. You can't have too much!"

Kevin asks Mari if he can have some
mangoes because her tree is so full.

It's his favourite too.

She didn't feel like sharing. So she told him he could come back tomorrow, maybe.

Why does Mummy wants to spoil her fun? She loves mangoes, she is not hurting anyone.

It will be alright if she just had one.

OK, maybe just one more teeny, tiny one.

It feels like there's a washing machine in her belly as it spins and grumbles. Time to go lie down.

She felt so ill. She couldn't believe she would miss the party tomorrow.

Mummy said, " Too much of a good thing is not always a good idea. If we only tried one thing, we would miss out on all the other great things to try like coconut fudge or skateboarding? When we try different things, we appreciate and enjoy what we like even more."

Mummy was right. She was sorry that she had been greedy. It made her feel bad when she had too much.

The next day, Mari was feeling better so she made some special deliveries.

Because everything tastes sweeter when you share.

The end

Author bio

Marva Carty is British born, Caribbean bred and US /UK educated. She has worked in fields such as university admissions, travel and tourism, children's toys, product marketing and internal communications. Her interests include zumba, gameshows and sharing bad puns. You can find her at www.mangolimepublishing.com

CPSIA information can be obtained
at www.ICGtesting.com
Printed in the USA
BVHW021644151121
621687BV00018B/933